SUNSET KEY

BLAKE CROUCH

RAVEN BOOKS
an imprint of
ORCA BOOK PUBLISHERS

Library and Archives Canada Cataloguing in Publication

Crouch, Blake
Sunset key / Blake Crouch.
(Rapid Reads)

Also issued in electronic format.
ISBN 978-1-4598-0253-7

I. Title. II. Series: Rapid reads
PS3603.R68S86 2013   813'.6   C2012-907307-5

First published in the United States, 2013
Library of Congress Control Number: 2012952477

Summary: When Letty Dobesh sets out to steal an expensive painting
from a wealthy convicted felon on one of his last nights of freedom,
she gets a good deal more than she bargained for.

MIX
Paper from
responsible sources
FSC
www.fsc.org   FSC® C016245

*Orca Book Publishers is dedicated to preserving the environment and has
printed this book on Forest Stewardship Council® certified paper.*

Orca Book Publishers gratefully acknowledges the support for
its publishing programs provided by the following agencies:
the Government of Canada through the Canada Book Fund and the
Canada Council for the Arts, and the Province of British Columbia
through the BC Arts Council and the Book Publishing Tax Credit.

Design by Teresa Bubela
Cover photography by Getty Images

ORCA BOOK PUBLISHERS
PO Box 5626, Stn. B
Victoria, BC Canada
V8R 6S4

ORCA BOOK PUBLISHERS
PO Box 468
Custer, WA USA
98240-0468

www.orcabook.com
Printed and bound in Canada.

16 15 14 13 • 4 3 2 1

CHAPTER ONE

Letty Dobesh came in from the cold to the smell of cooking eggs, bacon and stale coffee. The Waffle House was in College Park, a bad neighborhood in south Atlanta near the airport. She wore a thrift-store trench coat that still smelled of mothballs. Her stomach rumbled. She scanned the restaurant, dizzy with hunger. Her head throbbed. She didn't want to meet with Javier. The man scared her. He scared a lot of people. But she had $12.23 in her checking account, and she hadn't eaten in two days. The allure of a free meal was too much to pass up.

She had come twenty minutes early, but he was already there. He sat in a corner booth with a view of the street and the entrance. Watching her. She forced a smile and walked unsteadily down the aisle beside the counter. The points of her heels clicked on the nicotine-stained linoleum.

Sliding into the booth across from Javier, she nodded hello. He was Hispanic with short black hair and flawless brown skin. Every time they met, Letty thought of that saying, "the eyes are the windows to the soul." Because Javier's weren't. They didn't reveal anything—so clear and blue they seemed fake. Like a pair of rhinestones, with nothing human behind them.

An ancient waitress sidled up to their table with a notepad and a bad perm.

"Get ya'll something?"

Letty looked at Javier and raised an eyebrow.

He said, "On me."

"The farmer's breakfast. Extra side of sausages. Egg whites. Can you make a red eye? And a side of yogurt."

The waitress turned to Javier.

"And for you, sweetie?"

"Sweetie?"

"What would you like to order, sir?"

"I'll just eat her fumes. And a water."

"Ice?" The way she said it, it sounded like *ass*.

"Surprise me."

When the waitress had left, Javier studied Letty.

He said finally, "Your cheekbones look like they could cut glass. I thought you'd come into some money."

"I did."

"And what? You smoked it all?"

Letty looked at the table. She held her hands in her lap so he wouldn't see the tremors.

"Let me see your teeth," he said.

3

"What?"

"Your teeth. Show me."

She showed him.

"I'm clean now," she whispered.

"For how long?"

"A month."

"Don't lie to me."

"Four days."

"Because you ran out of money?"

She looked toward the open grill. She was so hungry she could barely stand it.

"Where are you staying?" Javier asked.

"Motel a few blocks away. It's only paid for through tomorrow."

"Then what? The streets?"

"You said you had something for me."

"You're in no condition."

"For what, a beauty pageant? I will be."

"I don't think so."

"Jav." She reached across the table and grabbed his hand. He looked down at it and then up at her. Letty let go like she'd touched a burning stovetop. "I need this," she whispered.

"I don't."

The waitress returned with Javier's water and Letty's coffee, said, "Food'll be right up."

"It's only day four," Letty said. "Another week, I'll be as good as new. When's the job?"

"It's too big to risk on a strung-out *puta*."

Anyone else, Letty would have fired back with some acid of her own.

Instead, she just repeated her question. "When is it?"

"Eight days."

"I'll be fine. Better than."

He watched her through those unreadable eyes. Said finally, "Would you risk your life for a million-dollar payday? I'm not talking about getting caught. Or going to prison. I mean the real chance of being killed."

Letty didn't even hesitate. "Yes. Javier, have I ever let you down?"

"Would you be sitting here breathing if you had?"

Javier looked out the window. Across the street stood a row of storefronts. A pawnshop. A hair salon. A liquor store. Bars down all the windows. There was no one out under the gray winter sky. The roads had already been salted in advance of a rare southern ice storm.

"I like you, Letty. I'm not sure why."

"You're not going to ask me why I do this to myself—"

"I don't care." He looked back at her. She could see he'd made a decision. "Letty, if you fail me—"

"Trust me, I know."

"May I finish?" He reached into his water and plucked out a cube of ice. Pushed it around on the table as it slowly melted. "I won't even bother with you. I'll go to Jacob first. And when you see me again, I'll have a part of him to show you."

She drew in a sudden breath. "How do you know about him?"

"Does it matter?"

The last two months of this crystal bender, she hadn't allowed herself to think about her son. He'd been taken from her just prior to her last incarceration. He lived in Oregon with his father's mother. Six years old. She pushed the thought of him into that heavy steel cage inside her chest where she carried more than a little hurt.

The food came. She wiped her eyes.

She tried not to eat too fast, but she had never been hungrier in her life. It was the first time she'd had real food in her stomach in days. Waves of nausea swept over her. Javier reached across the table and stole a strip of bacon.

"Bacon tax." He smiled and bit it in half. "Have you heard of a man named John Fitch?"

She didn't look up from the scrambled eggs she was shoveling into her mouth. "No."

"He was the CEO of PowerTech."

"What's that?"

"A global energy and commodities company based in Houston."

"Wait, maybe I did see something about it on the news. There was a scandal, right?"

"They cooked the books, defrauded investors. Thousands of PowerTech employees lost their pensions. Fitch and his inner circle were behind it all. A month ago, he was convicted for securities fraud. Sentenced to twenty-six years in prison."

"What he deserves."

"Says the thief. He's out on a seventy-five-million-dollar bail. Scheduled to report to a federal prison in North Carolina in nine days."

Letty set her fork down and took a sip of black coffee. She hadn't had caffeine in weeks, and already she was feeling jittery. "Where's this going, Jav?"

"Fitch's family has abandoned him. He has no one. He's sixty-six and will very likely die in prison. I happen to know that he's looking for some female companionship for his last night of freedom. Not a call girl from some—" Letty was already shaking her head "—high-end escort service. Someone very, very special."

"I'm not a prostitute," Letty said. "I've never done that, never will. I don't care how much money you wave in my face."

"Do you think I couldn't find a woman who is younger, more beautiful and more… *experienced*…than you if all I wanted was a hooker?"

"Charming."

"Letty, this could be the score of a lifetime for you."

"I'm not following."

Javier smiled, a terrifying spectacle.

The entire restaurant shook as a jet thundered overhead.

"It's not a trick," he said. "It's a heist."

CHAPTER TWO

The last work Letty had done with Javier had involved stealing from high rollers in Vegas. He'd hooked her up with universal keycards and supplied surveillance to let her know when marks had left their rooms. That job had presented a degree of risk for sure, but nothing beyond her comfort level. Nothing like this.

She cut into a waffle, said, "Gotta be honest—I'm not over the moon about the word *heist*."

"No? It's one of my favorites."

"It sounds like something you need a gun for. And a getaway car. The type of job where people get killed."

She swabbed the piece of waffle through a pool of syrup and took a bite.

"See, that's the beautiful thing about this job, Letty. It's high return on a low-risk venture."

"You just asked me if I'd be willing to *risk my life* for a million-dollar payday."

"I didn't say there was no risk. Just that it's low considering the potential payout."

"Do you have any idea how many times I've heard that and then the opposite proved to be—"

"Are you accusing me of glossing over risk in our prior dealings?"

Letty realized with a jolt of panic that she'd insulted him. Not a wise course. Javier didn't get angry. He just killed people. The stories she'd heard were the stuff of legend.

"I guess not." She backtracked. "It's just that I've been burned in the past. But not by you. You've always been on the level with me."

"I'm glad you see that. So would you like to hear me out, or should I leave?"

"Please continue."

"Fitch is spending his last days on his private island fifteen miles south of Key West. Most of his property has been lost to forfeiture to pay back the victims. However, I have a man in Fitch's security detail. He tells me there's something of great value at Fitch's residence in the Keys."

The waitress stopped at the booth and freshened up Letty's coffee.

When she was gone, Letty stared across the table at Javier.

"Well, do I have to guess?" she asked.

He glanced around the restaurant as he reached into his leather jacket. The sheet of paper he pulled out had been folded.

Javier slid it across the table. Letty pushed her plate aside and opened it.

She stared down at a painting printed in full color from a Wikipedia page—a skull with a burning cigarette in its mouth.

"What's this?" Letty asked.

"*Skull with Burning Cigarette*. You familiar with your post-Impressionists?"

"Not so much."

"You don't recognize the style?"

"I'm a thief, not an art collector."

"But you have heard of Vincent Van Gogh..."

"Of course."

"He painted this one in the mid-eighteen-eighties."

"Good for him."

"The original is hanging in Fitch's office in the Keys."

"Get to the good part."

Letty managed to smile through her driving headache.

13

"When we discuss the value," Javier said, "we're talking about two numbers. First, what could we sell it for at auction? In nineteen-ninety, Van Gogh's *Portrait of Doctor Gachet* sold for eighty million. In adjusted dollars, that's a hundred and forty."

Letty felt something catch inside her chest. It was a strange sensation, like being dealt four aces. She fought to maintain her poker face.

"You said there were *two* numbers?" she asked.

"Obviously, we can't just steal this painting and put it up for a public auction through Sotheby's."

"Black market?"

"I already have a buyer."

"How much?"

"Fifteen million."

"What did Fitch pay for it?"

"Doesn't matter. We're selling it for fifteen. You're rolling your eyes over fifteen mil? Really?"

"I just think we can—"

"You have no idea what you're talking about. Look at me." She looked at him. "You don't know me well. But from what you do know, do you honestly believe I would broker a deal for anything less than the most favorable payout to me? To my crew?"

When she didn't respond right away, he continued, "The answer you're looking for is 'no.' That should leave you with one question."

"What's my cut?"

"Two."

It was more money than Letty had ever imagined acquiring in a lifetime of theft, but she forced herself to shake her head. Strictly on principle of not accepting a first offer, if nothing else.

"No?" Javier seemed amused. "Two isn't a fair cut for a tweaker?"

"That's not even fifteen percent of the take, Jav."

"You think it's just you and me on this deal? That there aren't some other people I have to pay off? You wouldn't even have this opportunity without me. Sounds like you'd be living in a box somewhere."

"Why do you need me? Why not have your guy on the inside handle this?"

"That was the initial plan, but he was let go last week."

"Why?"

"Nothing related to this."

"So you *had* a man on the inside."

"This can still work, Letty. I can get you on that island with all the tools, all the intel you'll need."

She sighed.

"What?" he asked. "What are you thinking?"

"I'm thinking you might have put this together, but I'll be taking on most of the risk."

Javier cocked his head as if he might disagree.

Instead, he held up four fingers and then waved her off before she could respond. "I know it's hard for you, but just accept graciously, Letty. It'll buy you enough crystal to kill yourself a thousand times over."

"Go to hell."

Javier reached into his jacket again and tossed a blank white envelope on the table.

Letty opened the flap, peered inside.

A bunch of fifties and an airline ticket.

"You fly down to Miami a week from today," Javier said. "I'll be there to pick you up. There's a thousand in there. I assume that'll cover you until then?"

"Yeah."

She didn't even see his arm move. Suddenly, Javier had a grip on the envelope. She instinctively pulled back, but he wouldn't let go.

"Just so we're clear," he said, "this is for your room and board. And to get yourself a world-class makeover. Keep receipts for every purchase. If you use this money to buy meth…If you look anything like the car crash that's sitting across the table from me when you get off the plane in Miami…You know how this will end."

CHAPTER THREE

Letty walked back to her motel through the falling sleet. It made a dry, steady hiss drumming against the sidewalk. It was bitter cold. The streets were empty.

The thousand in her pocket kept whispering to her. *Take a detour down Parker Street. Score a teener. You'll still have time to get straight before Florida. You've got to celebrate. This could be the best thing that's ever happened to you. To Jacob.*

As she crossed Parker, she glanced down the street. Caught a glimpse of Big Tim standing on his corner, unmistakable in a giant down parka, designer jeans, fresh kicks.

She ached to score, but instead focused her gaze back on the road ahead.

Kept walking.

* * *

By the time she unlocked the door to her dingy motel room, Letty was freezing. She punched on the television and headed toward the bathroom. The local news was in hysterical storm-coverage mode.

She drew a hot bath. The tub filled slowly, steam peeling off the surface of the water. Letty stripped out of her clothes. She stood naked in front of the mirror hanging from a nail on the back of the door. A crack ran down through the glass. It somehow seemed fitting.

She'd never looked so thin. So haggard. In health, she was a beautiful woman with clear eyes the color of amber. Short, auburn hair. Curves in all the right places.

Now, the shape of her skeleton was emerging.

For a split second, Letty had the strong sense of her old self, her real self, her best self, trapped inside the emaciated monster staring back at her.

It took her breath away.

CHAPTER FOUR

One week later, Javier picked Letty up in a black Escalade curbside at Miami International. They headed south into the Keys on the Overseas Highway that crossed the 110-mile island chain. The stereo system blasted Bach's Four Lute Suites on classical guitar. Letty leaned her head against the tinted glass and watched the world go by.

Land and sea. Land and sea.

On the far side of Key Largo, Javier glanced across the center console.

He said, "You don't even look like the same woman."

"Amazing what a little mud rinse and a padlock can do."

"Your eyes are clear. Your color's good."

"I put on ten pounds since you saw me last. Got my hair and nails done. I did a whole spa thing yesterday. I wasn't sure what to wear for tomorrow…"

"I brought your dress. I brought everything you'll need."

Letty couldn't remember the last time she'd seen the ocean. More than ten years ago, at least. The sea was blue-green, and the sky straight blue and scattered with clouds that resembled puffs of popped corn. It was early afternoon. Short-sleeve weather. Winter felt like a word that had no meaning here.

They rode through Islamorada and Layton.

Quaint island villages.

Past Marathon, they crossed Seven Mile Bridge into the Lower Keys.

The views into the Gulf of Mexico and the Straits of Florida went on forever.

* * *

They reached Key West in the late afternoon, and Javier checked Letty into the La Concha Hotel. She tried to lie down but her mind wouldn't stop. She poured herself a merlot from the minibar and went to the table by the window. The breeze coming through the screen smelled like cigar smoke and sour beer. And the sea.

She sat drinking and watching the evening come.

Her room on the fifth floor overlooked Duval Street. It was crowded with cars and bicycles. Tourists jammed the sidewalks. She heard a ukulele playing in the distance. On many rooftops, people had gathered to watch the sunset. She wondered what it would feel like to be here on vacation. To have

no plans beyond finding a place for dinner.
To be in paradise with someone you loved.

*   *   *

She didn't have to see Javier until lunch the
next day, when they would make their final
preparations. So Letty slipped into a new
skirt and tank top and headed out into
the evening.

There was an atmosphere of celebration.

Everyone happy and loaded. Nobody
alone.

At the first intersection, she left the
chaos of Duval Street. Two blocks brought
her into a residential quarter. It was an old
neighborhood. She passed restored bunga-
lows and Caribbean-style mansions.

On every block, there was at least one
house party going.

Ten minutes from the hotel, she found a
Cuban restaurant tucked away in a cul-de-sac.

The hostess told her it would be a ninety-minute wait.

There was a patio out back with a tiki bar, and Letty installed herself on the last available stool.

The noise was considerable.

She didn't like being here alone.

She opened her phone and tapped out texts to no one.

It took five minutes for the barkeep to come around. He was an old salt—tall and thin. So grizzled he looked like he'd been here back when Hemingway hung around. Letty ordered a vodka martini. While the barkeep shook it, she eavesdropped on a conversation between an older couple seated beside her. They sounded Midwestern. The man was talking about someone named John and how much he wished John had been with them today. They had gone snorkeling in the Dry Tortugas. The woman chastised her husband for getting roasted in the sun, but he expertly steered the conversation away from himself. They talked about other places they'd been together. Their top three bottles of wine. Their top three sunsets. How much they were looking forward to a return trip to Italy. How much they were looking forward to Christmas next week with their children and grandchildren. These people had seen the world. They had loved and laughed and lived.

Letty felt a white-hot hate welling up in the pit of her stomach.

She didn't even bother to persuade herself it wasn't jealousy.

The barkeep set her martini down. A big, sturdy glass the size of a bowl. The drink had been beautifully made, with flakes of ice across the surface.

"Wanna start a tab?"

"No."

"Twelve dollars."

Letty dug a twenty out of her purse.

The barkeep went for change.

The gentleman beside her had worn a sports coat for the evening. In the light of the surrounding torches, Letty could see by the cut that it was designer. Gucci or Hugo Boss. She could also see the bulge of a wallet in the side pocket. So easy to lift. Two moves. Tip over her martini glass in the man's direction and slip her hand into his blazer pocket as he reached for a napkin to help clean up. She'd done it a dozen times, and only once did the mark ignore the spill.

And that'll really make you feel better? To drop a bomb on their holiday?

When she stole, it was out of necessity. Only ever about the money. She'd never made it personal. Survival had been her sole motivation, even at her lowest points. Never the intentional infliction of hurt to boost her own morale.

While the old barkeep was still at the register, Letty slipped off the chair, leaving her drink untouched.

She threaded her way between tables, out of the restaurant and onto the street.

By the time she reached Duval, she had managed to stop crying.

Her life seemed to be defined by moments like these.

Moments of pure self-hatred.

And this was just one more in a long, long line.

CHAPTER FIVE

"You slept okay?" Javier asked.

"Yes."

"How are you feeling?"

"All right. Nervous."

"Good."

"Good?"

"Nerves keep you sharp."

Wind rustled the fronds of the palm tree that overhung their table. They were sitting outside at a café two blocks from the ocean. A cruise liner had just unloaded gobs of people onto the island. They were streaming past on the sidewalk. Herds of Hawaiian shirts and panama hats propelled by pasty-white legs.

"You should eat something," Javier said.

Their waiter had brought their lunches five minutes ago, but Letty hadn't touched her ham-and-brie panini or her salad.

"I'm not hungry."

"Eat."

She started picking at her salad.

Between bites, she pointed the tines of her fork at the chair between them, where Javier had placed a cardboard box.

"Is that my dress?"

"Among other things."

"Is it pretty?" she asked in a mock-girlish voice.

He ignored this. "In the box, you'll find a mini spray bottle. The label says mouthwash. It's an opiate tincture. Oxycodone. Fitch is a wine snob. Five squirts in his wineglass during dinner. Not four. Not six. Exactly five."

"Got it."

"Get him to his room before he starts to fade. His people will hang back if they think you've gone in there to sleep with him."

"How thoughtful."

"Once he's unconscious, head up to the office. Now listen to me very carefully. My contact says there will be five men on the island. Three outside. Two in the residence. Considering his notoriety, Fitch has had countless death threats and one actual attempt. These men are private security contractors. Ex-Blackwater types. They've all seen combat. They'll be armed. You won't be."

"Where will you be during all this?"

"I'm getting there. Part of your outfit is a Movado watch."

"Ooohhh, Christmas."

"Don't get attached. It's on loan. We rendezvous at eight on the eastern tip of the island. You won't be allowed to bring your cell phone. Keep an eye on your watch."

He patted the box. "There's also a map of the island and blueprints of the house. I would've given them to you earlier, but I just got my hands on them."

"What if I get held up?"

"Don't get held up."

"Eight. All right. How are we getting off the island?"

"A Donzi Twenty-Two Classic Shelby. I'm picking it up after we're done here."

"Is that a boat or a plane?"

"It's a boat."

"Fast?"

"Faster than any of Fitch's watercraft. *Miami Vice* fast."

"Assuming this works, what'll stop them from just radioing for help? Having the coast guard track us down on the way back to Key West?"

"You are taking on some risk here, which is why I will tolerate these questions that seem to suggest I haven't thought everything through. That I haven't foreseen every possible glitch and planned accordingly." Javier took a sip from his glass of ice water. "We won't be going back to Key West. We'll be heading five miles farther south to a deserted key in international waters."

Letty forced herself to take a bite of the sandwich.

Javier said, "Now, we haven't even discussed the most important part of this. The reason we're all here."

"*Skull with Burning Cigarette.*"

"The painting is hanging in Fitch's office on the wall behind his desk. My intel is that there's no theft-security system. You just have to cut it out of the frame."

"Cut it?"

"Careful. Like shooting heroin into your femoral artery careful. There's a razor blade hidden on the bottom of your handbag, under a piece of black electrical tape."

"I'm not comfortable with that," Letty said.

"Why?"

"Because they'll probably search the handbag, don't you think?"

"Where do you want to hide it?"

"I'll think of something. What kind of bag is it?"

"Try to control yourself. Louis Vuitton."

"Up to this point, the accessories are far and away the best part of this job. Them, I keep."

"We'll see."

"And once I get the canvas out of the frame?"

"Roll it up. You'll find a plastic tube taped to the underside of Fitch's desk. Stick the rolled-up canvas inside and get yourself to the eastern edge of the island."

"What about cameras?"

"None."

"What about the people who actually see me up close? Who can identify me and describe me to law enforcement?"

"You'll be a redhead tonight."

"That's it?"

"What do you want, a latex mask? This isn't *Mission Impossible*. This is the price you pay for a shot at four million dollars."

Letty felt something go cold at the base of her spine.

Without exception, this was the most dangerous job she'd ever signed on for.

Javier said, "You wondering why I don't just slip in there while you're distracting Fitch?"

"Now that you mention it."

"Because that would turn this into a very different kind of job. People would die. I assume you don't want that."

"No."

Javier tossed his napkin onto the table. He stood and looked at his watch.

"It's almost two thirty. They're picking you up outside the hotel at four." He pulled out his money clip and dropped two twenties on the table. "Go back to your hotel. Study your maps. Get your head right for this."

Letty had barely touched her food.

Javier stared down at her through a pair of aviator sunglasses.

"You forgot something," she said.

"What's that?"

"My name. Who will they be expecting?"

"Selena Kitt. S-E-L-E-N-A-K-I-T-T. But you won't be carrying any identification."

"And my back story? Should he be so inquisitive?"

"Thought I'd leave that to you. Bullshit seems to flow so freely from your lips. Moments like this don't come along very often," he said.

"I know."

"Ship sails at four. Make me proud, Letisha."

CHAPTER SIX

Riding down to the lobby, Letty watched herself in the reflection of the elevator doors. So did the twenty-year-old boy with an obvious hangover standing beside her. She didn't blame him. She looked stunning. The little black dress was Chanel. The fuck-me pumps were Jimmy Choo. They made her legs look like stilts. She'd worn wigs before, but nothing as finely made as this one—wavy red hair that fell just past her shoulders. Javier certainly had a well-developed sense of style, but she couldn't imagine he'd put this ensemble together all by himself.

The elevator doors spread apart. Letty tried to steady her breathing as she walked out into the lobby past a grouping of palm trees in planters.

She glanced at her watch. Three fifty-eight.

As she approached the revolving door at the entrance, a man stood up from a leather chair. He wore a black suit and carried the beefy build of a bouncer. Bald, graying goatee and a sharp skepticism in his eyes. She figured the extra padding under his jacket for a shoulder holster.

"Ms. Kitt?"

"The one and only."

The man extended his hand, and she shook it. "I'm James. I'll be taking you to Mr. Fitch. Right this way."

He led her outside to a silver Yukon Denali idling on the curb and opened the rear passenger door. Letty climbed in. The driver didn't bother to introduce himself. He wore sunglasses and a black suit almost identical to James's. He was younger, with a buzz cut and a strong, chiseled jaw that Letty associated with soldiers.

The radio was tuned to NPR and turned down so low that Letty could barely hear it.

James sat beside her.

As they pulled out into traffic, he reached behind them into the cargo area and retrieved a black leather pad. He opened it and handed Letty a sheet of legal-size paper. At the bottom, she noticed a line for the signature of Selena Kitt.

"What's this?" she asked.

"A non-disclosure agreement."

"For what?"

"For anything that happens from the moment you climbed into this vehicle until you're returned to Key West."

She studied the document.

"Looks like a bunch of legalese."

"Pretty much."

"You wanna give me the CliffsNotes, since I didn't go to law school?"

"It says that you agree not to disclose any details regarding your time with Mr. Fitch. Not in writing. Not in conversation with anyone. And if you do, you can be sued for breach of contract in accordance with the laws of the State of Florida."

"You mean I can't write a tell-all book and then sell the movie rights about Mr. Fitch's last night of freedom?" She smiled to convey the intended humor, but James just tapped the signature line with a meaty finger.

"Sign right here, please."

* * *

They parked at a marina on the west coast of the island, not far from the hotel. Letty walked between her escorts to the end of a long dock. Waited for several minutes while the men took in the mooring lines on a fifty-foot yacht. When they'd prepped the boat for departure, the driver climbed to the bridge. James offered Letty a hand and pulled her aboard. He led her up several steps and through a glass door into a salon.

The pure luxury stopped her in her tracks and took her breath away.

"Please make yourself comfortable," James said, gesturing to a wraparound sofa.

Letty eased down onto the cool white vinyl.

"Would you care for a drink?" he asked.

She knew she shouldn't, but she felt so jittery she figured just one wouldn't hurt. Might even help to calm her down.

Letty peered around James at a wet bar stocked with strictly high-end booze.

"I see you've got Chopin," she said.

"Rocks?"

"Yes."

"With a twist?"

"No, thank you."

James crossed the teak floor to the freezer and took out a bucket of ice. Letty leaned back into the cushion and crossed her legs. The engines grumbled to life deep inside the hull. At the bar, James scooped ice cubes into a rocks glass and poured. He brought her drink over with a napkin.

"Thank you, James."

He unbuttoned his black jacket and sat down beside her.

She could feel the subtle rocking as the yacht taxied out into the marina.

There were windows everywhere, natural light streaming in through the glass. The view was of a colony of sailboat masts, the dwindling shoreline of Key West, and the sea.

Letty sipped her drink. The vodka was nearly flavorless in her mouth, with a slight peppery burn going down.

"That's very good." She set her glass on the coffee table.

"We need to have a conversation," James said.

"Okay."

"You're aware of who your client is?"

"Mr. Estrada explained everything to me."

"This is a very important night for Mr. Fitch."

"I understand that."

"And you're here for one reason, Ms. Kitt. To make it as special and as memorable as it can possibly be." Letty was nodding and trying to find a window to break eye contact. But James's stare held her. She couldn't help feeling they were the eyes of a cop. Hopefully an ex-cop. "There are a few topics of conversation that are off-limits," he continued. "You are not to bring up the case against Mr. Fitch, his trial or his conviction in any way. You are not to discuss his sentence or anything relating to the prison term he's facing."

"Okay."

"You will not discuss anything you've read in the papers or on the Internet. You will not discuss your view of his guilt or innocence."

"I have no views. No opinions whatsoever."

"Now I need you to stand up for a minute."

"Why?"

"Just do it, please."

Letty uncrossed her legs and stood.

James got up as well and faced her.

"Hold your arms out."

"Are you frisking me?"

"That's exactly what I'm doing. Mr. Fitch has received numerous death threats since the case against him was filed."

"And you think I'm hiding something in this itty-bitty dress?"

"Hold your arms out horizontal to the floor."

Letty did as she was told and stared out the window while James patted her down, his hands roving over every nook and cranny.

45

"Jesus, at least buy me dinner first."

"All right, you can sit, but I will need to search your purse."

Letty handed over the Louis Vuitton.

The yacht exited the marina. The engines roared to life as they throttled out into open water. She could feel the tension in her gut ratcheting up a notch. Having never learned to swim, being surrounded by water always made her uneasy.

She tried not to watch too intently as James opened the handbag. He removed the contents, one at a time, and lined them up on the coffee table.

Lipstick.

Mascara.

Package of Kleenex.

Hotel keycard.

He paused as he lifted out the mini spray bottle.

"What's this?" he asked.

Letty's heart stomped in her chest.

"Just what it says. Breath freshener."

James held it up to the light and read the label. "Watermelon?"

"Try it, if you like."

James let slip a tight smile and set the bottle on the table. Then he dumped out the remaining items—a condom, a mirror, brush, gum and two hair bands.

"You left your cell phone. Good."

James held the interior of the handbag up to the window so the sunlight could strike the black textile lining.

After a moment of close inspection, he handed her the bag and said, "I apologize for the intrusion. We should be arriving in less than twenty minutes."

James walked out of the salon. She heard him talking quietly into his cell phone.

Letty returned everything to her purse and settled back into the sofa with her glass. She sipped her drink and turned her thoughts to this man she would be spending the coming hours with. From everything she'd read, including the verdict forms, Fitch was a monster. His conspiracy and fraud had resulted in the bankruptcy of PowerTech. Fifteen thousand employees had lost their jobs. Many had lost their life savings. Investors in PowerTech had lost billions.

Throughout his prosecution, Fitch had maintained that he just wanted the chance to tell his story. But at crunch time on the witness stand, he'd invoked the Fifth Amendment to avoid self-incrimination.

The yacht hummed along at forty knots, skimming the water like a blade across ice.

Key West was nothing but a blurred line of green on the horizon.

Out here, there was nothing but the sea, in all its varying hues of blue and jade. Its surface sparkled. The horizon was sprinkled with tiny islands. The sky shone a deep, cloudless blue. It was early evening. They cruised straight into a red and watery sun.

Letty could feel the vodka buzz coming on like a soft warmth behind her eyes. A numbness in her legs. For a fleeting second, everything seemed so impossibly surreal.

This yacht.

This thing she was about to do.

This life she lived.

CHAPTER SEVEN

The sea in the vicinity of Fitch's island was shallow. His dock extended seventy-five yards out from the shore into water deep enough to berth a boat.

Letty followed James out of the salon onto the stern.

A tall thin man stood on the last plank of the dock. He was throwing squid into the sea, his gray hair blowing in the breeze. He wore a white, long-sleeved shirt unbuttoned to his sternum. White Dockers. Leather sandals. He was darkly tanned. He finished rinsing off his hands under a faucet mounted to the end of the wharf and dried them with a towel as Letty approached. Reaching down, he gave her a hand up onto the dock. He was even taller than she'd first thought. Six-two. Maybe six-three. He smelled of an exotic cologne—sandalwood, spice, jasmine, lime, money.

The man still hadn't let go of her hand. His fingers were cool and moist, as soft as silk.

"Welcome to Sunset Key, Selena. Please call me Johnny."

She could hear Texas in his voice, but it wasn't overbearing. Houston drawl by way of an Ivy League education. She stared up into his face. Smooth-shaven. No glasses. Perfect teeth. He didn't look sixty-six years old.

"It's beautiful here, Johnny," she said.

"I like to think so. But it pales in comparison to you. They broke the mold."

Letty's eyes riveted on what he'd been feeding—gray fins slicing through the water.

"Sand sharks," Fitch said. "Not to worry. Totally harmless. They like the reefs for protection. A mother and her pups."

He offered his arm. They walked down the long dock. Letty could see the cupola of a house peeking above the scrub oak that covered the island. According to the blueprints and to Javier, that was Fitch's office.

"How was your ride over?" Fitch asked.

"Wonderful. Your yacht is amazing."

"Part of my midlife crisis, some would say."

Letty glanced back over her shoulder.

James and the unnamed driver followed at a respectful distance.

"Don't give them another thought," Fitch said. "I know James searched you, and I apologize for that barbarous invasion, but it couldn't be helped."

"It was no big deal," she said.

"Well, you're *my* guest now."

"I'm glad to hear it," Letty said. "You've lived here long?"

"Back in my former life, I was primarily based in Houston. I also had a winter place in Aspen. An apartment in Manhattan. Of course, those are gone now. But I bought this key twenty-two years ago when it was fourteen acres of unspoiled paradise. Designed the house myself. It was always my favorite. There's a view of the sea from every room."

They went ashore.

A man of fifty or so stood waiting for them in khaki slacks and a short-sleeved button-down.

"Selena, this is Manuel, my caretaker and steward. He's been with me for…how long, Manuel?"

"Since you buy island. I live here almost twenty-two years."

Fitch said, "Before we go to the house, I thought we'd take a walk on the beach." He kicked off his sandals.

Manuel turned to Letty. "If you give me shoes, I take them up to house for you."

Letty leaned over and unfastened her pumps. She stepped out and handed them to Manuel.

"And your purse?"

"I think I'll hang on to this."

Fitch said, "Thank you, Manuel."

"Very good, sir."

"You're leaving for Key West when Angie goes?"

"Yes, I go with her."

"Take care, my old friend."

Letty and Fitch walked barefoot up a man-made beach.

"Manuel came over on a raft. Half of them died. Sends his paychecks back to Havana. He's an honorable man. Loyal. He'll never have to work again after tomorrow. He doesn't know this yet."

The sand was soft and stark white and still warm from the sun. There was no surf, no waves. No boats within earshot. Letty could hear the sound of leaves rustling, a bird singing in the interior of the island, and little else. The water was bright green.

Fitch picked up a shell before Letty stepped on it.

He said, *"Down on the seashore I found a shell, / Left by the tide in its noonday swell / Only a white shell out of the sea, / Yet it bore sweet memories up to me / Of a shore where brighter shells are strown, / Where I stood in the breakers, but not alone."*

"That's lovely," Letty said.

They moved on up the shore. It seemed that with every passing second, the sun expanded, its pool of light coloring a distant reef of clouds.

"It's why I chose the Keys, you know," Fitch said. "Best sunsets in the world. Ah. Here we are." They had reached the tip of the island. A pair of adirondack chairs waited in the sand under the shade of a coconut palm.

They faced west, an ice bucket and a small, wooden box between them.

Letty and Fitch crossed the sand to the chairs. The sunset spread across the horizon like a range of orange mountains. There was no wind. The water was as still as glass.

Letty glanced down at the box. The top had been stamped:

HEIDSIECK & CO. MONOPOLE

GOÛT AMÉRICAIN

VINTAGE 1907

NO. 1931

Fitch pulled an unlabeled bottle out of the ice water. He held it to the fading light. The glass was green and scuffed. He went to work opening it.

Letty said, "Special. Even has its own box."

"This bottle was on its way to the Russian royal family when the boat carrying it was torpedoed by Germans. What must have gone through those young sailors' minds? It took a half hour. They knew, for a half hour, they were going to die and could do nothing to stop it. Nothing but wait and watch the minutes slide."

"In what year?"

"Nineteen-sixteen. The vintage is nine-teen-oh-seven, which makes this—"

"Ninety-eight years old?"

He nodded.

"Oh my god."

"It was recovered from the wreck seven years ago. The bottles were perfectly preserved at the bottom of the ocean. Notable not only for the rarity and the history—as it turns out, the wine itself is quite excellent. I bought one for a special occasion. I'd say tonight qualifies. Would you get the glasses, please?"

Letty reached into the box and lifted out two crystal flutes.

"Go ahead and ask," Fitch said as he struggled with the cork.

"Ask what?"

He worked it out so slowly, there was no *pop*. Just a short *hiss* as the pressure released. The cork crumbled in his hand. He held the opening of the bottle to her nose.

It smelled like perfume.

"What do you think?" he asked.

"Gorgeous."

Fitch took a whiff himself and then began to pour.

"So ask," he said. "It won't offend me."

"What?"

"What I paid."

"That would be rude."

"But you want to know."

With her glass full, Letty smelled it again, the carbonation bubbles misting her nose.

"All right. What'd you pay, Johnny?"

"Two hundred and seventy-five thousand dollars. Here's to you," he said.

She didn't even know how to comprehend such a figure...for a single bottle of wine!

"To you, Johnny."

They clinked glasses.

The champagne was amazing.

"I want to know your passion, Selena."

"My passion?"

"What is it that most excites you in this life? What is your prime mover? Your reason for being here?"

"Prada."

This got a huge laugh.

"Money can't buy you happiness, darling. Believe me, I've tried."

"But it affords your own brand of misery."

"You're a lively one, Selena. That's good. Real good. Let's sit back and enjoy, shall we?" Fitch said. "This is going to be a night for the senses."

Letty leaned back in her chair. "That's the prettiest sunset I've ever seen," she said.

"I'm just glad it didn't rain." Fitch laughed, but there was a sadness in it.

All the color went out of the sky.

"Where are you from, Selena?" Fitch
asked.

Letty had only had two glasses, but she
felt good. Too good. "A little bit of everywhere. I guess I don't really think of any one
place as home."

Fitch looked over at her. He patted her
hand.

"I know this must be a strange deal for
you," he said.

"It's not."

"You're kind to say that, but..." He stared
out across the sea. With the sun gone, there
were only shades of blue. "I'm just really glad
you're here tonight."

* * *

They walked toward the house on a sandy
path that cut through the heart of the island.

Letty held Fitch's hand.

"You have a real sweetness about you,
Selena," he said. "Reminds me of my wife."

"You miss her? No, I'm sorry. That's not my business."

"It's all right. I brought her up. Yeah, I miss her. She left me a year and a half ago."

"Before your trial."

"Go through something like this, you find out real quick who your friends are. It's not always your kin. Only real loyalty I've seen is from Manuel and my lawyers. Both of whom I pay. So what does that tell you? Two of my sons won't speak to me. My youngest only communicates by email. I understand to a point, I guess. I've put them through a lot. Do you have children, Selena?"

"I have a son," Letty said before it even crossed her mind to lie.

"Is he in your life?"

"He's not."

Through the underbrush, Letty caught a glimpse of house lights in the distance.

Fitch said, "But is there anything he could do that would make you stop loving him?"

"No."

"Anything that would make you willingly abandon him?"

"Absolutely not."

"I suppose our kids don't love us quite like we love them."

"I hope that's not true."

"I've had my fair share of company over to the island. You're different, Selena."

"I hope you mean that in a good way."

Fitch stopped. He turned and faced her and pulled her body into his.

"I mean it in the best way."

It took her by surprise when he leaned down for a kiss.

Not the kiss itself, but the pang of guilt that ripped through her like a razor-tipped arrow.

CHAPTER EIGHT

The house was a large gray box set on foundation piers. It had long eaves and wraparound decks on the first and second levels. Extensive lattice-work enclosed the space under the stairs. Letty spotted rafts and plastic sand-castle molds. Snorkeling gear. Life jackets. Beach toys that she imagined hadn't been touched in years.

She and Fitch rinsed the sand off their feet at the bottom of the stairs.

Halfway up, Letty could already smell supper cooking.

As they walked through the door, Fitch called out, "Smells wonderful, Angie!"

Letty followed him into an open living space. Hardwood floors. Exposed timber beams high above. The walls covered in art deco. A giant marlin had been mounted over the fireplace. A live jazz album whispered in the background. There were candles everywhere. The bulbs in the track lighting shone down softer than starlight.

"You have a lovely home, Johnny."

Letty spotted James and another man walking down a corridor. She and Fitch passed a spiral staircase. They arrived at a granite bar that ran the length of the gourmet kitchen. A stocky woman in a chef coat slid something into a double oven. She wiped her brow on her sleeve and came over.

"Selena, meet Angie," Fitch said.

"Hello," Letty said.

"Angie is head chef at a Michelin-starred restaurant in Paris. I flew her over to prepare something special for tonight. How's it coming, Angie?"

"I can bring out starters whenever you're ready."

Fitch glanced at Letty. "Hungry?"

"Starving."

"We're ready," he said.

"How about wine?"

"Yes, I think we'd like to have some wine. You decanted everything I showed you?"

"They're in the cellar, ready to go. What would you like to start with?"

"Bring out the nineteen-ninety Petrus, the 'eighty-two Château Lafite Rothschild and the 'forty-seven Latour a Pomerol."

"Quite a lineup," Angie said.

"So much good wine to drink, so little time. We'd like to taste everything side by side, so bring six glasses."

"You aren't trying to get me drunk, are you?" Letty teased, bumping her shoulder into Fitch's arm.

"Now why would I need to do that?"

They sat at an intimate table in a corner, surrounded by windows.

In the candlelight, Fitch looked even younger.

Letty dropped her handbag on the floor between her chair and the wall.

Angie brought the wine in three trips, carrying the empty bottle in one hand and a crystal decanter in the other.

All of the Bordeaux was astonishing. With wine like this in the world, Letty didn't know how she could ever go back to seven-dollar bottles of Merlot from the supermarket.

They started with a plate of plain white truffles.

Then foie gras.

Then scallops.

Angie kept bringing more courses. Because Letty was drinking out of three glasses, she had difficulty gauging her intake.

She tried to pace herself with small sips, but it was simply the best wine she'd ever tasted.

Over the cheese course, Fitch said, "It occurs to me there will be many evenings to come when I long to return to this meal."

Letty reached across the table and took hold of his hand.

"Let's try to stay in the moment, huh?"

"Sound advice."

"So, Johnny. What is your passion?"

"My passion?"

"For a man who has achieved all the material wants."

"Experience." His eyes began to tear. "I want to experience everything."

Angie came over to the table. "How was everything?"

"I'm speechless," Fitch said.

He rose out of his seat and embraced the chef. Letty heard him whisper, "I can't thank you enough for this. You're an artist, and the memory of this meal will sustain me for years to come."

"It was my pleasure, Johnny. Dessert will be up in fifteen."

"We're done here, and we can handle getting dessert for ourselves. Someone will clean up. You've been cooking all day. Why don't you take off?"

"No, let me finish out the service."

"Angie." Fitch took hold of her arm. "I insist. Pete's waiting in the yacht to take you back."

For a moment, Letty thought Angie might resist. Instead, she embraced Fitch again, said, "You take care of yourself, Johnny."

Fitch watched her cross to the front door.

As she opened it, she called out, "Dessert dishes and silverware are on the counter beside the oven! Goodnight, Johnny!"

"'Night, Angie!"

The door slammed after her, and for a moment, the house stood absolutely silent.

Fitch sat down.

He said, "How strange to know you've just seen a friend for the last time."

He sipped his wine.

Letty looked out the window.

The moon was rising out of the sea. In its light, she could see the profile of a suited man walking down a path toward the shore.

"It begins to go so fast," Fitch said.

"What?"

"Time. You cling to every second. Savor everything. Wish you'd lived all your days like this. Excuse me."

He rose from his seat. Letty watched him shuffle across to the other side of the room and disappear through a door, which he closed after him.

She lifted her purse into her lap and tore it open. Her fingers moved with sufficient clumsiness to convince her she'd gotten herself drunk. She grasped the spray bottle. Fitch still had some wine left in two of his glasses.

Reaching across the table, she put five squirts into the one on the left.

The door Fitch had gone through creaked open.

He emerged cradling a bottle in one arm and carrying two glasses in the other.

He was grinning.

From across the room, he held up the bottle, said, "The jewel of our evening. Come on over here, sugar."

Fitch sat down on a leather sofa.

Letty still hadn't moved, her mind scrambling.

I missed my chance. I missed my chance.

CHAPTER NINE

Fitch waved her over. "Sit with me!"

Letty glanced at her watch as she stood. Seven-oh-five.

Fifty-five minutes until her rendezvous with Javier at the east end of the island.

She grabbed one of her wineglasses and Fitch's.

He was already tugging the cork out of the bottle as she walked over.

Letty said, "Here you go and leave, and I was just on the verge of making a beautiful toast." She tried to hand Fitch his wineglass.

"We'll toast with this instead," he said, showing her the bottle—Macallan 1926.

"Oh, I'm not too much of a scotch girl."

"I understand, but this is really something. You couldn't *not* love this."

"Now I'm losing my nerve."

She thought she registered a flash of something behind his eyes—rage? But they quickly softened. Fitch put the bottle down and accepted his glass and stood.

Letty had no idea of what to say.

She looked up at Fitch and smiled, her mind blank.

It came to her in an instant—a toast she'd overheard at a wedding she'd crashed two years ago. Back then, she'd spent her Saturdays stealing presents from brides and grooms. She'd developed something akin to an X-ray sense for determining the most expensive gifts based solely on wrapping paper.

She raised her glass.

"Johnny."

"Selena."

"May a flock of blessings light upon thy back."

"Ah, Shakespeare. Lovely."

Letty watched as he polished off the last two ounces of his wine. They sat on the sofa. Fitch opened the scotch and poured them each two fingers into heavy tumblers.

He put his arm around Letty. She cuddled in close. He went on for a minute about the rarity of this spirit they were about to imbibe. He was drunk, beginning to ramble. She finally sipped the scotch. It was good. Better than any whiskey she'd ever tasted, but she hadn't lied. She just wasn't a scotch girl.

After awhile, he said, "Everything I've ever done, I've done for my family, Selena. Everything."

Sitting with Fitch on the sofa, it hit her again. That old, familiar enemy. Regret. Guilt. Her conscience. Truth was, she liked Fitch. If for no other reason than he was facing a lifetime behind bars with grace.

Making the most of his final hours of freedom. She tried to remind herself of all the people Fitch had hurt. And it wasn't like he'd be hanging this painting she was about to steal on the walls of his prison cell.

But the arguments rang hollow. Insincere.

After a while, she felt his head dip toward hers.

He was saying something about his family, about how everything had always been for them. His eyes were wet. He didn't sound drunk so much as sleepy.

Letty set her glass on the coffee table and eased Fitch's out of his grasp.

"What're you doing?" he slurred.

Letty stood and took him by the hand. She pulled him up off the couch.

"Come with me," she whispered.

"My drink." His eyes were heavy.

"You can always finish your drink." She pressed up against him and wrapped her arms around his neck. "Don't you want *me*,

Johnny?" She kissed him with passion this time—open-mouthed and long. Hoped it would give him enough of a charge to make it into bed.

She led him through the living room.

"Where's your room?" she whispered, even though she knew from the blueprints that it was very likely the large master suite on this level. He pointed toward the opening to a hallway just behind the spiral staircase.

They stumbled down a wide corridor. The walls were covered with photos of Fitch's family. One in particular caught Letty's eye as she passed by. It had been taken out on the deck of this house fifteen, maybe twenty, years ago—a much younger Fitch standing with three teenage boys. All shirtless and tanned. Mrs. Fitch in a bathing suit. The sea empty, huge and glittering behind them.

Letty dragged Fitch through the doorway of his bedroom and shut the door behind them. The suite was sprawling. There was a flat-screen television mounted to the wall across from the bed. A bookcase. A small desk, where she spotted a laptop, cell phone and empty wineglass. Floor-to-ceiling windows looked out over the dock. French doors opened onto the deck. She couldn't see the moon from here, but she could see its light falling on the sea.

"Go lie down," she said.

Fitch staggered toward the bed.

Letty took her time pulling the curtains.

Fitch mumbled, "You're so…beautiful."

"That's what my daddy used to tell me." She could feel the rush of adrenaline cutting through her intoxication. "I just need to step into your bathroom for a moment," she said. "I'll be right out. You get comfortable."

He said, "We don't have to do anything. Unless you want to." The words came too soft, too muddled.

Letty walked into the bathroom. She shut the door, hit the light.

It was bigger than most apartments she'd lived in. Leaning over the sink, she studied her pupils in the mirror. They were black and huge. She sat down on the toilet and took a deep breath. All the things she needed to do in the next forty-five minutes pressed down on her. She took herself through all the steps. Pictured it happening perfectly.

Five minutes passed.

She went to the door.

Pulled it open as softly as she could manage and slipped back into Fitch's room.

The wood-paneled walls now glowed with a soft warmth from candles on the bedside tables. They smelled like vanilla. The hardwood creaked as she crossed to the foot of Fitch's bed.

The old man lay on his back with his arms and legs spread out. His shirt was unbuttoned, his pants pulled down to his knees. It was as far as he'd gotten. He snored quietly, his chest rising and falling.

He looked tragic.

"Bye, Johnny," Letty whispered.

Then she moaned several times.

Full-voiced and throaty.

Hoping that would keep Fitch's men away from his room for the time being.

CHAPTER TEN

The bedroom door opened smoothly, without a sound. She moved in bare feet down the corridor. All of the doors she passed were cracked. The rooms, dark. Where the hallway opened into the main living area, she stopped. The spiral staircase was straight ahead, but hushed voices crept around a blind corner. It sounded like they were coming from the kitchen. For a moment, she stood listening. Two men. They were eating, probably picking through the leftovers.

Letty went quietly up the staircase, taking the steps two at a time.

Near the top, she caught a view down into the kitchen. It was James and some other black-suited man with long hair who she hadn't seen before. They stood at the counter, dipping crackers into the foie gras.

She came to the second floor. A long hallway, empty and dark, branched off from either side of the spiral staircase. The blue-prints had indicated that this level housed four bedrooms, two bathrooms and a study. Letty kept climbing, using the iron railing as a guide. The noise of the men in the kitchen fell farther and farther away. By the time she reached the final step, she couldn't even hear them.

Letty stepped into the cupola of the house.

Because three of the walls consisted entirely of windows, the moonlight poured inside like a floodlight.

Letty ripped off the wig. She ran her hands carefully through her hair until her fingers found the razor blade.

Padding over to the desk, she turned on a lamp.

Her watch read 7:45.

She stared up at the wall above the desk.

What the hell?

She'd been expecting to see the Van Gogh—a skeleton smoking a cigarette. What hung on the wall was an acrylic of a horse. Maudlin colors. Proportions all wrong. She was no art critic, but she felt certain this painting was very badly done.

Leaning in close, she read the artist's signature in the bottom right-hand corner of the canvas.

Margaret Fitch.

Letty sat down in the leather chair behind the desk. Her head felt dizzy and untethered. Had Javier told her the wrong place to look?

Had she somehow misunderstood him? No, this was Fitch's office. In fact, there should be a plastic tube taped beneath the desktop. She reached under, groping in the darkness. All she felt was the underside of the middle drawer.

Assumptions.

Somewhere, she'd made a false one.

The blueprints had identified the cupola as an office, but maybe Fitch's was actually down on the second floor.

That had to be it.

She spun the swivel chair around and started to rise.

Took in a hard, fast breath instead.

A shadow stood at the top of the spiral staircase, watching her.

CHAPTER ELEVEN

For a long minute, Letty couldn't move. Her heart banged in her chest like a mental patient in a rubber room.

"Dear old Mom did that one," Fitch said, "God rest her soul." He pointed to the painting of the horse behind his desk. "She gave it to me for Christmas fifteen years ago. I hated it at the time, and with good reason. Let's be honest. It's hideous. So I kept it in a closet, except for when she visited. Then I'd have to swap out my Van Gogh for that monstrosity. Make sure she noticed it proudly displayed in my office."

"Johnny…"

"And then she died, and I got sentimental. I sold *Skull with Burning Cigarette* and put *My Horse, Bella* on that wall permanently. It's been there for five years, and every time I look at it, I think of my mother. I've even come to appreciate certain aspects of it."

Fitch took a step forward into the splay of light emanating from the desk lamp. He looked clear-eyed. He held a large-caliber revolver in his right hand. His glass of Macallan in the other.

"There are similarities between you and Van Gogh, Letisha. Both fiery redheads, with a nasty predilection for self-injury. Suffering from what the psychoanalysts would best describe as daddy issues. And perhaps most pityingly, both masters of a trade you would never be appreciated for. At least, not in life.

"You look confused, Letty." Fitch smiled. "Yes, I know your real name. I like it more than your alias, if you want to know the truth. Although I did prefer you as a redhead."

He sipped his scotch.

"Did you call the police?" she asked.

He laughed. "I'm going to see my fair share of law enforcement for the rest of my life, don't you think? The notion that you'd try to steal from me? Come onto my island and steal from me? You brazen girl."

"Johnny." Letty thought she might be just drunk enough to scare up some real emotion. She had disarmed her fair share of men in the past with a few tears.

"Oh, don't cry, Letty."

"I'm sorry, Johnny. I tried to take advantage of you, and—"

"No, no, no. I should be the one apologizing to you."

She didn't like the sound of that. Something in the tone of his voice suggested a piece of knowledge she wasn't privy to.

"What are you talking about?" she asked, starting to get up.

"No, you just stay right there, please."

She settled back into the chair.

"My life," Fitch said, "has been so rich. So...fragrant. I went to Yale undergrad. Harvard business. I was a Rhodes scholar. Earned a PhD in economics from Stanford. I lived in Europe. The Middle East. Argentina. I rose as fast through the ranks of PowerTech as anyone in the history of the company."

Fitch edged closer, his hair trembling in the breeze stirred up by a pair of ceiling fans.

"By thirty-five, I was the youngest CEO of a global energy company in the world. I had a family I loved. Mistresses on six continents. I was responsible for twenty-four thousand employees. I brokered multibillion-dollar deals. Destroyed both domestic and foreign competitors. I've fucked in the Lincoln bedroom under three separate presidencies. I've been adored. Demonized. Admired.

Copied. I've played hard. Made men and ruined men. Had the finest of everything. More money than God. More sex than Sinatra. Trust me when I say I go to federal prison for the rest of my life a happy man. If the masses knew how much pure fun it is to have this kind of power and wealth, they'd kill me or themselves."

He walked to one of the windows and stared out across the moonlit sea.

"You're a beautiful woman, Letty Dobesh. In another life...who knows? But I didn't allow you to come into my home for sex. I've had plenty of that." He held up his tumbler. "And I don't really even care about this forty-thousand-dollar bottle of single malt. On the last night of a man's life, before he reports to prison for a twenty-six-year stint that will likely kill him, he has to ask himself, What do I do with these last precious moments? Do I revisit the things in life that most made me happy?

Or use this last gasp of freedom to have a truly new experience?"

Letty eyed the staircase.

If she hadn't been drunk, she could've probably reached the steps before Fitch turned and fired. But he was holding a beast of a gun. A .44 Magnum or worse. Taking a bullet from something of that caliber would finish her.

"What does this have to do with me?" she asked.

Fitch turned and faced her.

"Sugar, there's one thing I've never done. I was too old for the draft in nineteen-sixty-nine. I've never been to war, which means I've never had the experience of taking a life."

"He'll kill you," she said. "Even in prison, he can get to you."

"Are you talking about Mr. Estrada?"

She nodded.

"You don't see it yet, do you?"

"See what?"

"It was Javier who put this whole thing together, Letty. There was never any painting. No drug in your mouthwash spray. I told him about this last experience I wanted to have before I went away, and for a very significant price, he brought you to me."

Letty felt a surge of hot bile lurch out of her stomach—anger and fear.

She fought it back down.

"Johnny..."

"What? You going to beg me not to do this? Try to test the limits of my conscience? Good luck with that."

"It won't be how you think. It's not some great rush."

"See, you don't understand me. I have no expectations of feeling one way or another. I just want to have done it. What's a richly lived life that has never caused death? You ever killed someone, Letty?"

"Yes."

"How was it?"

"Self-defense."

"Kill or be killed?"

She nodded.

"Well, how was it?"

"I think about it every day."

"Exactly. Because you had a true experience. And that's all I want. This is how it'll work. I'm going to wait right here for five minutes. Give you a head start. See, I don't just want to kill you, Letty. I want to hunt you."

"You're as evil as they say."

"This is not about good and evil. I've lived dangerously all of my life. I want to continue to do so on this final night, when it counts the most. My security team is on their way down the dock as we speak. They're going to anchor my speedboat a quarter mile out. My yacht is staying in the marina in Key West for the night. It'll just be you and me on the island. I know you can't swim, Letty. That was one of the requirements that, unfortunately for you, landed you this job. So there are no ways off this little island."

"I have a son," she said.

"Haven't we covered that already?"

"Johnny, please." Letty stood up slowly and moved forward with her arms outstretched, hands open. "Has it occurred to you that you aren't thinking clearly? That you have all this emotion swarming around inside of you and—"

Fitch pointed the revolver at her face and thumbed back the hammer.

"That's close enough." It wasn't the first or the second or even the third time she'd had a firearm pointed at her. But she'd never got used to that gaping black hole. Couldn't take her eyes off it. If Fitch chose to pull the trigger in this second, it was the last thing she'd ever see.

"You destroyed thousands of lives," she said, "but you aren't a murderer, Johnny."

"You're right. Not yet. Now you have four minutes."

CHAPTER TWELVE

Letty raced down the spiral staircase.

Drunk.

Terrified.

Still trying to wrap her head around what had just happened.

Only one conclusion. Javier had played her.

Sold her out.

She passed the second floor and ran down the remaining steps into the living room. Straight to the cordless phone on a bookshelf constructed from pieces of driftwood. She grabbed the handset off its base, punched *Talk*.

Fitch was already on the other end of the line. "I'm afraid that's not going to work, Letty. Three minutes, thirty seconds. Twenty-nine. Twenty-eight…"

I need a weapon.

She dropped the phone and turned the corner into the kitchen. She started yanking drawers open.

As she pulled open the third, she saw it lying on a butcher-block cutting board next to a pile of onion and garlic skin. A chef's knife with a stainless handle and an eight-inch blade.

For ten seconds, she stood in the remnants of Angie's cooking, trying to process her next move. So much fear coursing through her, she felt paralyzed.

There were dishes everywhere.

A tart cooling on the granite beside the oven.

Water dripping from the faucet.

Every second slipping by like the prick of a needle.

Fitch expected her to run. To chase her across the island. So should she stay in the house? Hide in a bedroom on the second floor and let him wander around outside in vain?

Decide. You can't just keep standing here.

Grabbing the knife, she bolted across the room into the foyer. Jerked open the front door. Slammed it shut after her. She shot down the steps, wondering which way to go. The shore seemed like a bad idea. She headed into the interior of the island, staying off the path, fighting through the undergrowth. Gnarled branches clawed at her arms. Ripped tears in her Chanel dress. Her bare feet crunched leaves and tracked through patches of dirt. She'd barely made it fifty yards when a blinding pain seared the sole of her right foot.

Letty went down, clutching it.

In the moonlight that filtered through the leaves, she studied the damage. The underside of her foot had been starred with a dozen sandspurs. She began pulling them out one at a time. Wincing. Wondering how many minutes she had left. Less than two? Less than one?

The sound of the front door creaking open on its salt-rusted hinges answered her question.

She looked up.

All she could see was the top half of Fitch standing on the deck. When he reached back to shut the door, she noticed that he wore a strange-looking hat. He moved out of view, the steps groaning as he descended.

Letty dug the last few spurs out of her foot.

She could hear Fitch approaching.

Footsteps and heavy breathing.

She didn't move.

Figured Fitch had to be walking up the path. It didn't sound like he was thrashing through undergrowth.

Letty inched back farther into the shadow of the scrub oak. Tucked her chin into her knees and tried to make herself as small as possible.

Fitch passed within twenty feet.

She crouched there listening until his footfalls could no longer be heard.

Letty crawled out from under the oak and came to her feet.

Total silence.

The stars shining.

The moon still climbing in the sky.

She knew what the shore on the dock side of the island was like from that sunset stroll. A narrow strip of beach lined with vegetation. No place to hide.

She moved slowly through the scrub oak, taking care that her shoulders didn't brush against the branches. She crested the midpoint. The island sloped gently down to the opposite shore. This side struck her as more wild. There was no beach. Just mangroves all the way down to the water.

She squeezed her way through the slim trunks. The mangroves grew more densely clustered as she neared the shore. Letty crawled on hands and knees now. The foliage above her head so thick, it blotted out the sky. Only splotches of moonlight scattered across the ground.

She went on until the trees were too close to go any farther.

They boxed her in like prison bars.

Lying on the ground, her body twisted between the mangroves, she finally breathed deep and slow.

The temperature hovered in the upper sixties, but she was shivering, covered in sweat. Her dress had been shredded as she climbed through the mangroves. It hung from her shoulders in tatters.

She felt good about this spot. Considering that it was dark, she was all but invisible. And Fitch would have a hell of a time reaching her. She couldn't imagine the old man, who had at least ten inches on her, fitting through this grove of tightly packed trees. How big had he said this island was? Fourteen acres? Best-case scenario, she could hole up here for the night. Fitch had to report to prison tomorrow. If she could survive until then...

Letty glanced at her watch. The tips of the hour and minute hands glowed in the dark.

Seven thirty.

She should've been meeting Javier at the east end of the island with fifteen million dollars in a plastic tube. This should've been the most exhilarating, life-changing score of her life. Instead, she was being hunted down like a dog. Because she'd put her faith in a psychopath. Because, again, her judgment had failed.

Something niggled at her.

A seemingly small fact she was overlooking.

A rodent scurried through some leaves nearby.

A mosquito whined in her ear.

What was it?

No flashlight.

That was it.

Fitch hadn't brought a flashlight outside with him. When she'd glimpsed him walking down the steps, she'd expected to see a light wink on. But it never did. And then he'd just strolled up that path in the dark like—

Her breath caught in her chest.

Like he could see.

She sat up.

That wasn't a strange-looking hat he'd been wearing. Those were night-vision goggles.

Thirty, forty yards away—impossible to know for sure—Letty heard branches rustling.

It was the sound of something big coming her way through the underbrush.

Get out of here now.

Letty started pushing her way through the labyrinth of mangroves. By the time she broke free onto higher ground, her little black dress dangled from her by a thread.

An oak branch beside her face snapped off.

The gunshot followed a microsecond later.

A *boom* like a clap of thunder.

And she was running.

Arms pumping.

Gasping.

Driven by pure instinct.

She ducked to miss an overhanging branch, but another one caught her across the forehead.

Blood poured down into her face.

She didn't stop.

There were lights in the distance.

The house.

She veered toward it. At least inside, Fitch wouldn't have the sight advantage he held right now.

Letty came out of the scrub oak and onto the dirt path that cut down the middle of the island. For three seconds, she paused. Hadn't had this much physical exertion in months. Her lungs screamed. She could hear Fitch closing in.

Letty opened up into a full sprint as she approached the house.

She reached the stairs, grabbed the railing.

Three steps up, she stopped. Maybe it was a premonition. Maybe it was just a feeling. Something whispered in her ear. *You go in that house, you won't ever come out alive.*

She backed down the steps and stared into the darkness under the stairs. *Where is the last place in the world he would expect someone to hide who can't swim?* She thought.

Her eyes fell upon the snorkel set hanging from a nail driven into the concrete.

She grabbed the snorkel and mask and took off running toward the east end of the island—the only side of it she hadn't seen.

She shot back into the scrub oak. Glancing over her shoulder, she spotted Fitch coming into the illumination of the flood-lights mounted to the deck. He pulled off the goggles to pass through the light. Held them in one hand, that giant revolver in the other. A big, sloppy grin spreading across his face like a kid playing cowboys and Indians.

Another fifty yards through the oaks, and then Letty was standing on the shore in her strapless bra and panties. Her Chanel had been ripped off completely.

The water looked oil-black.

She could hear Fitch coming.

Wondered how much time she had.

Wanted to do anything but wade out into the sea.

CHAPTER THIRTEEN

Letty pulled on the mask and stepped into the water. It was cool, just south of seventy-five degrees, and shallow. She took invisible steps, no idea if the next would plunge her in over her head or shred her feet on coral.

By the time she'd gone thirty feet out from the shore, the water came to her knees. At fifty feet, it reached her waist. She stopped, couldn't force herself to take another step. Hated the feel of it all around her, enclosing her. Reminding her in so many ways of death.

Fitch stumbled out of the oaks and onto the beach. He stood profiled in the moonlight. He was looking all around as Letty jammed the snorkel into her mouth and slowly lowered herself into the sea. Struggling not to make a splash or a ripple.

The water rose above her chest.

Then her neck.

Up the sides of her face.

Daddy, please.

She could breathe, but still she felt as though she were drowning. No sound underwater but her own hyperventilation as she sucked air down the tube at a frantic pace.

Her knees touched the sandy bottom of the ocean floor.

The claustrophobia was unbearable.

Even with her eyes wide open, she couldn't see a thing.

Lifting her right arm, she fingered the top of the snorkel. It stuck two inches out of the water. She pushed with her knees, rose up slowly until the top half of the mask peeked above the surface.

Fitch still stood on the shore, staring in her direction.

She dipped back under.

It was unbearable.

Nine years old.

The cool and the dark of it.

By herself at night in the singlewide trailer she shares with her father. He comes home from the bars. Drunk and angry and alone. He loves to take hot baths when he's drunk, but Letty has beaten him to it. He finds her soaking. With their water heater on its last leg, it will take two hours to heat enough for another bath. In a rage, he shatters the fluorescent bulb over the sink and locks her inside. Tells her through the door that if she gets out of that bath before he says she can, he'll drown her in it.

It's wintertime. Four hours later the water is cold and the air temperature in the bathroom even colder. Letty sits with her knees drawn into her chest, shivering uncontrollably. She's crying, calling for her father to let her out. Pleading with him for forgiveness.

Toward dawn, he kicks the door in. From the smell of him, he's somehow drunker than before.

She says, "Daddy, please."

It happens so fast. She doesn't even see him move. One minute she's shivering and staring up at him. The next, he's holding her head under the frigid bathwater, telling her what a bad girl she is to make him so angry. He's beaten her before. He's come after her with a broken beer bottle. With his belt. With his fists. With other things. But she has never believed she was going to die.

Because there was no warning, she didn't have a chance to take in a full breath of air. Already, bright spots are blooming behind her eyes, and she's struggling, kicking. Wasting precious oxygen. But his boot heel presses down hard against her back. Pinning her to the fiberglass. He holds her head down with two hands.

Even drunk, he has the strength of an ox. The build of a diesel mechanic. She is no match. Every second passing so slowly. Panic setting in. Thinking, He's going to kill me. He's really going to kill me this time.

The fear and the horror meet in a single, desperate need. Breathe. Breathe. Breathe. *She can't help it. Can't resist the pure, burning desire. She takes a desperate breath just as her father jerks her head out of the water by her hair.* "Think you learned a lesson?" *he growls.*

She nods, apologizing as she bawls hysterically out of the only emotion her father has ever caused in her—fear.

There are other nights like this. A handful of them are worse. She will never learn to swim. Will always fear the cold, dark water. Will never understand, despite a thousand sleepless nights, why her own father hated her.

And, like that nine-year-old girl, a part of her still believes it was her *fault. Some flaw in her emotional chemistry. And nothing she can do, no amount of logic, no quantity of love from anyone, will ever make her stop believing it.*

Letty came up suddenly out of the ocean.

If Fitch saw her and shot her, so be it. But she couldn't stand another second underwater.

He was gone.

She spit out the snorkel's mouthpiece. Took several careful steps toward the shore, until the water level had dropped to her thighs. She stared down the north and south beaches. It was too dark to see much of anything.

Backing away again, she settled down into the water until only her head was above the surface.

Waited.

Five minutes slipped by.

Twenty.

It was beyond quiet.

She watched the moon on its arcing path over the island.

So thirsty. Her head pounded from the booze.

After a long time, she heard footsteps.

Letty backed into deeper water and lowered herself once more until only her eyes were exposed.

Fitch trudged up the north beach and arrived at the end of the island. He stopped and waited, listening.

Letty forced herself back under.

When she came up a minute later, Fitch had started down the south side of the island.

Fitch has to report to prison tomorrow. If I can survive until then...

She returned to that comforting thought she'd had in the mangroves. The idea that if she survived until tomorrow, until Fitch was gone, she would be in the clear.

Is this another assumption that's going to get me killed?

Fitch's security detail had played a part in this. Exactly how much they knew was uncertain, but they were culpable. Fitch's life would be over tomorrow, but theirs would carry on. If the old man didn't close the deal, could she really expect this force of ex-military contractors to leave this loose thread dangling?

Another impulse of fear swept through her.

A new realization setting in.

Hiding all night from Fitch might not be enough to save her life.

CHAPTER FOURTEEN

Letty stood up and walked out of the sea, the taste of salt water on her tongue. When she reached the shore, she pulled off the mask and dropped it and the snorkel in the sand. She gripped the knife. Headed quickly down the south beach. The fear fell away, anger rushing in to fill the void.

She could see Fitch in the distance, his white shirt bright as day in the moonlight. He walked sixty yards ahead, but she was gaining on him. She kept close to the trees that lined the beach in case Fitch suddenly spun around. Her footfalls in the soft white sand were soundless. She picked up her pace, moving now at a full run. The wind blowing her skin dry. The faster she ran, the angrier she got, the less afraid she felt.

Fitch was only twenty yards ahead of her now. Her legs ached from the full-on sprint. Her lungs burned. Tears streamed out of the corners of her eyes.

She knew exactly what had triggered it.

Being down under that cool, December water.

How could she not think of Daddy? Dead twenty years, yet still with her. Always with her. She'd heard somewhere that every person reaches a certain age and, though they keep getting older, never feels any older.

In so many ways, she was still that nine-year-old girl shivering in cold bathwater.

In prison, she'd sat through enough AA and NA meetings to know the drill.

The propaganda.

Admit a lack of control.

Acknowledge a higher power.

Make amends.

Embrace forgiveness.

That was all fine and good. But at the end of the day, the nine-year-old trapped in this woman's body could care less about twelve steps. Her world was imbalanced in the worst possible way—she'd had a monster for a father. If she lived to be a hundred, she would never get over it.

Up ahead, Fitch was almost to the dock.

Letty slowed from a sprint to a jog, trying to mask her accelerated breathing.

She leapt over a piece of sand-blasted driftwood.

Took the final steps slow and careful.

Fitch held the revolver in his right hand. His gait looked tired, like an old man's.

Letty tightened her grip on the knife and pushed the point of the blade into his back.

Fitch took a sudden breath and quit walking.

She said, "I'll shove it through to your stomach. Drop the gun...I swear to God."

He still held the gun. Letty leaned her weight into the blade, and as it started to penetrate, the revolver hit the sand.

She lunged down for the gun, and let go of the knife as she picked it up.

Stumbled back away from Fitch.

The revolver was a giant thing. Must have weighed four or five pounds. It was nickel-plated and over a foot long. *Raging Bull* was engraved down the side of the barrel.

Letty had to struggle to keep it leveled on Fitch's chest.

"You just stay right there," Letty said, backing another foot away.

Four cartridges remained in the cylinder.

"You lost your lovely dress," Fitch said.

"Get down on your knees."

Fitch carefully lowered himself into the sand. "That's a big gun for a little girl. Packs a helluva kick."

It took her two fingers to pull the hammer back.

"Wasn't personal," Fitch said, the pitch of his voice kicking up a few degrees. "I hope you understand that. You are a formidable little girl. A scrapper. In another life, I'd have you come work for me."

"Why is that all I ever hear anytime somebody does me wrong? Nothing's ever personal anymore. All those people you ripped off...that wasn't personal either, was it? Just business, right?"

"Letty—"

"No, you've explained yourself plenty. Your men are offshore in boats?"

"Yes."

"Are there any other boats on the island?"

"No."

"Do you have your cell phone with you?"

"No."

"We're going to the house."

"Why?"

"Get up. Start walking."

"Calling the police would be a very bad idea, Letty."

"Get. Up."

Slowly, Fitch stood.

"Now walk over to the dock," she said. "And do it slowly, with your hands raised."

But Fitch didn't move. He just stared at her.

"Do you think I'll tell you again?" she asked.

"I knew. I knew it all along. From the minute I met you. That this would be one hell of a night, Letisha. Rare to feel I've met my match."

He let slip a long, tired breath.

Like he'd come to the end of something.

Then sprang at Letty.

It was the loudest gunshot she had ever heard, with a kick like a shotgun.

Fitch sat in the sand. His mouth dropped open. He made a sucking sound, as if trying to draw breath. The hole in the dead center of his chest was massive. Letty was shaking. Fitch fell back onto the beach and stared up at the stars. There was so much blood, she knew he was going to die.

Out on the water, a motor growled to life.

Letty turned around. She looked down the dock and out to sea.

A single spotlight glided toward her, the motor getting louder as it approached. Soon she could see the profile of the speedboat. It was seconds away from reaching the end of the dock.

CHAPTER FIFTEEN

Letty sprinted inland. Already she could hear men's voices behind her. Shouting her name. Her real name. Ordering her to stop as their shoes pounded against the planks.

She tore up the steps onto the deck and shouldered her way through the front door.

After several hours in the dark, the onslaught of light made her eyes water.

Letty barged into the living area and rushed to the cordless phone. It was still lying on the floor where she'd dropped it. She grabbed it, hit *Talk*, held it to her ear.

Beep-Beep-Beep-Beep-Beep-Beep-Beep-Beep...

She raced down the hallway into Fitch's bedroom.

Slammed the door after her, locked it, flipped the lights.

Thank god.

There it was.

Lying on the desk.

She picked up Fitch's cell phone and flipped it open, praying it still held a charge.

Outside, she could hear numerous sets of footsteps hammering up the stairs.

Men screaming her name.

They charged into the house.

Hide.

Letty crossed the hardwood floor to the french doors.

Someone was coming down the hall.

She turned the handle.

Locked.

The knob on the other door rattled— someone trying to get in.

She was out of time.

Nothing left to do but fight.

Three bullets versus three or four men.

This may be how it ends for you. Are you ready?

The door splintered, a man kicking it in from the other side.

She aimed the revolver at the bedroom door.

After two more kicks, the door burst open, and the muscled girth of James filled the doorway. His cheeks were flushed from running. With one arm, Letty trained the Raging Bull on his substantial center mass. In her other hand, she gripped the cell phone.

Her thumb keyed in 9-1-1.

James held a black pistol at his side. At least for the moment, he was smart enough to keep it there.

Someone on the second floor yelled his name.

"Down here!" he shouted back.

"You got her?"

"Sort of!"

Letty moved her thumb toward a green icon on the cell phone's keypad that she assumed would initiate the call.

As the other men came running, James said, "Who you calling?"

"Nine-one-one."

"Why don't we talk about that, okay?"

Letty's right biceps had begun to cramp from holding the Raging Bull with one hand.

She could hear the other men in the hallway now.

James yelled over his shoulder, "Everybody stay back!"

"What exactly do we have to talk about?" she asked.

"How dialing that number is going to get you killed."

"Way I figure, I'm dead either way."

"That's not true. But if you involve the Monroe County Sheriff's Department, we're going to have a problem. Why don't you put that gun down? I'll do the same. And we'll talk."

"I'm not putting anything down. You people tried to kill me."

"What if I were to guarantee your safety?"

"I'd call bullshit."

"You put the gun down. I'll get you some clothes. And I'll have you back on Key West within the hour."

"You must think I'm really stupid."

"No, ma'am." He shook his head. "This can work out for everyone. Of course, you'd have to do a few things for me."

"Like?"

"Like never mention any of this to anybody. Ever."

"What about that famous dead man on the beach? Aren't some people expecting him tomorrow?"

"We can damage-control the mess you made of Mr. Fitch."

"The mess I made."

"It's you I'm worried about."

Over James's shoulder, Letty spotted a man creeping into view.

"Your buddy right behind you is about to get you shot, James."

"Go sit in the living room!" he yelled. "All of you!"

"James—"

"Right now, Scott."

She heard them falling back.

James looked at her. "Better?"

"For some reason, I don't think you'd be so interested in talking to me if I didn't have this big goddamn hand cannon pointed at your chest."

"Now that's just not true. You put it down and see."

"I don't think so. Tell me again how you're planning to 'damage-control' your boss."

"If all goes well," James said, "if you and me don't have a big shootout, you'll see some breaking news tomorrow morning.

It'll go something like this…convicted CEO of PowerTech found dead on his private beach. He took his own life the night before he was scheduled to report to prison. There will even be a suicide note."

"Oh, you can fake his handwriting too?"

"No, he already wrote it."

Letty's strength was failing. She didn't want to, but she set the cell phone on the floor at her feet and took a two-handed grip on the revolver.

"Asking yourself why he might've done such a thing?" James asked. "Regardless of what you may think of him, Fitch is a brilliant man. He saw this as a possible outcome of what he had planned for tonight. He didn't want anyone to take the fall. Not me or the other guys. And not even you, the woman who killed him."

"Prince of a man."

James patted his lapel pocket. "I've got his note right here."

"That's a pretty story," Letty said. "And you're a world-class con man."

"Call my bluff. Put that gun away and see. I've got a lot of work to do before the sun comes up."

"I'm thinking if I put this gun down, you'll do one of two things. Shoot me straightaway and bury me on this island. Or take me out into some deep water. Dispose of me there."

"I can certainly understand you thinking the worst. All things considered."

"So then, how can you honestly believe I'd ever put this gun down with you still breathing?"

"Because when you think it through, you'll see there's no other way. Maybe I'm lying. You've got three rounds left in that Taurus. You'd kill me. No doubt. If you got really lucky, you might kill one of my other men. But the third? And the fourth? They'd take you down. And you know this. The thing is, if you shoot me, you'll never find out if

I'm lying or telling the truth. 'Cause you'll be dead. In fact, I don't want to alarm you, I don't want you to make any sudden moves, but there's a man standing on the deck right behind you. He's pointing a three-fifty-seven at your head through one of the panes of glass. And he could've fired sixty seconds ago."

Letty exhaled a long, slow breath.

She hadn't heard any footsteps on the other side of the french doors.

It was a smart play on James's part. Get her to turn her head. Distract her just long enough to raise his weapon and fire.

James was smiling now.

Letty's palms were sweating so badly the grip of the revolver was dripping.

"So what do you say, Letty? Doesn't some part of you want to know if I'm actually this good of a liar?"

"Not really."

She squeezed back the hammer.

The moment her finger touched the trigger, there was the sound of wood splintering and glass breaking behind her.

The gun fired as someone crashed into her back with devastating force.

She went down hard, crushed under the weight of a man with foie gras on his breath. Footsteps raced down the hallway, the other men pouring into Fitch's bedroom.

She struggled, but it was no use. He had her pinned to the hardwood floor and the gun lay just out of reach.

The man on top of her said, "James, you hit?"

"Just a graze across my shoulder. Damn if that wasn't close though."

Letty's eyes welled up as she felt him jerk her wrists behind her back and bind them together with a Zip Tie.

"Quit fighting me, sweetheart," the man whispered into Letty's ear. "It's over. You're done."

CHAPTER SIXTEEN

The noise of the powerboat engines was deafening.

Letty's hair whipped across her face, but she couldn't brush it away, with her hands still bound behind her back. James was at the controls, and she sat in the bucket seat behind him, next to the man who'd taken her down. He was the oldest of Fitch's security crew. Forty-five or fifty with shoulder-length hair the color of dishwater.

The sun wasn't up yet, but the first light of dawn had begun to color the eastern sky.

She shivered. She could feel goosebumps rise on her bare arms.

Waiting for the engines to go silent.

Dreading it.

Of all the ways to die, considering her past, she feared drowning more than anything. Would they tie something around her to weigh her down? Then just throw her over the side?

She would beg for a bullet when the time came.

And if they don't oblige you?

They would *have* to. She'd do whatever it took. She couldn't allow herself to be tossed overboard while still alive. Couldn't spend her last three minutes sinking into the cool, dark sea. Fighting that terrible thirst for oxygen as it swelled up inside her lungs. Meeting the same death her daddy had almost given her.

The panic grew.

She could feel herself beginning to come apart at the seams.

And then…

Lights shone in the distance.

* * *

James throttled down as they approached the marina.

He guided the boat into an open slip and killed the engines.

He got up and faced Letty.

"Stand up," he told her.

She stood.

The man beside her pulled out a folding knife and cut her wrists free.

James reached to the copilot seat and grabbed a wad of clothes. He handed them to Letty.

"You're letting me go," she said.

James nodded.

"But you let me believe you were going to—"

"You tried to kill me, Ms. Dobesh. My shoulder is still burning. If I were you, I would put those clothes on right now and get the hell out of my boat."

*   *   *

Letty moved through the lobby of the La Concha Hotel. Despite the wreck she must have looked, the concierge still smiled and nodded as she stumbled past.

She wasn't drunk anymore. Just tired to the point that nothing seemed real. Not the planted palm trees or the chandeliers. Not the eerie quiet of 5:00 AM. Not even her own reflection in the elevator doors as she rode up to her room.

She drifted down the corridor like a vagabond. Old pair of flip-flops. Boxer shorts. A Jimmy Buffett T-shirt from Fitch's closet that had faded into oblivion. She couldn't even think about the last ten hours. They were beyond processing.

Morning was almost here.

She had no money, no idea how she would get back to the mainland.

But one thought kept needling her.

Javier.

The strangest thing was that his betrayal didn't just make her angry. It hurt her too. It wasn't like he was a friend. She couldn't believe that Jav was even remotely capable of experiencing the feelings it required to maintain a friendship.

And yet...it hurt.

They had worked together two times before. Both had been successful. So why had he done this to her?

She shoved her keycard four times into the slot before the light on the door blinked green.

Because he's a psychopath, Letty. He had a need. You filled it. End of story.

She kicked off the flip-flops and staggered toward the bed.

Smelled his exotic cologne a half second before she noticed Javier sitting at the small table by the window.

She brought her hand to her mouth.

The door whisked closed behind her.

In a night of being chased and shot at, none of those horrors could touch the sheer terror of seeing Javier Estrada sitting like a demon in her hotel room.

She stood frozen, wondering if she could get out the door before he stopped her.

"You wouldn't make it," he said. "Please." He motioned to the bed. "I'm sure you're very tired."

Letty sat down on the edge of the mattress and put her face in her hands.

She said, "Oh god."

So many times tonight, she had thought she was going to die and didn't.

Now this.

After everything.

It was too much.

"What do you want to ask me?" he said.

She made no response.

"Nothing? How about...am I surprised that you are not dead?"

"You son of a bitch." She muttered it under her breath.

"Ask me," he said.

She glared over at him. "Are you surprised I'm not dead?"

"I am not," he said.

"Good for you." Her eyes were filling up with tears. "Good. For. You. Why didn't you just let Fitch's men kill me? Wanted to clean up this last little detail yourself?"

"I like you, Letty."

"Has anyone ever told you you're deranged?"

Javier opened a laptop sitting on the table beside a Slimline Glock.

He said, "You may choose to believe I betrayed you. I don't see it that way."

"Really."

He began typing, still watching her out of the corner of his eye.

"There were reasons I couldn't tell you the true nature of the job. It partly had to do with promises I made to our client, Mr. Fitch. But some of it just came down to my faith in you." He stared at her. "Two times before this, we worked together. I've seen you in action. Simply put, you're a survivor. I believed you would survive tonight."

"You had no right to—"

"And yet I did. Next topic. Part of my agreement with Mr. Fitch was that if you survived, if you killed him, his men were not to touch you. I went so far as to promise him that if anyone other than him laid a hand on you, I would kill his men and his sons too. Was a hand laid upon you?"

"Why didn't you just let me in on this?"

"Because you might've said no. Come over here. I want to show you something."

Letty stood, slowly, awkwardly. Already her legs had gone stiff.

Three feet away from him, she stopped.

"What?" she asked.

Javier was pointing at the laptop. "Do you see this?"

She leaned over his shoulder, squinting at the screen.

It was an accounts page on a website for the First National Bank of Nassau.

"What's this supposed to be?" Letty asked.

"It's an account I opened for you. Do you see this?"

Javier was pointing at a number.

$1,000,000.

"Is that…"

"Yes. That's your balance. Do you remember the first thing I asked you when we met back in Atlanta?"

"You asked if I'd risk my life for a million-dollar payday."

"And do you recall—"

"I said yes."

"You said yes. I know I said four million, but I wasn't even paid four for this job. I'm giving you fifty percent. You earned it."

Javier stood.

He stared down at her through those alien-blue eyes.

"You know to keep your mouth shut about Fitch."

Letty nodded.

Javier lifted his Glock and jammed it into the back of his waistband. He picked up his leather jacket, slid his arms carefully into the sleeves.

"Why are you giving this to me?" Letty asked.

"Who can say? Maybe we'll work together again."

"You still sold me out."

"You'll get over it. Or you won't."

He walked out.

Letty sat at the table and stared at the computer screen for a long time. She couldn't take her eyes off that number.

Light was coming into the sky. The lights along Duval Street were winking off. She couldn't imagine falling asleep now.

Letty raided the minibar and stocked her purse. Headed out still wearing John Fitch's clothes.

The roof of the hotel was vacant.

The bar closed.

Letty eased down into one of the east-facing deck chairs.

Drank cheap champagne.

Watched the sun lift out of the sea.

Something Jav had said kept banging around inside her head. *It'll buy you enough crystal to kill yourself a thousand times over.* Already she was feeling the itch to score. A pure craving. Is that what lay in store? Three months from now, would she be living out of another motel? Ninety pounds and wasting away? Now that she had enough money to finish the job, would she use until her teeth melted and her brain turned to mush?

Until her heart finally exploded?

She told herself that that wasn't going to happen, that she wouldn't lose control again, but she didn't know if she believed it.

The sun climbed.

Soon there were other people on the roof and the smell of mimosas and bloody marys in the air.

Letty ordered breakfast.

As the morning grew warm, she thought about her son.

In better times—mostly while high—she had imagined sweeping back into Jacob's life. Saw them in parks. Parent–teacher conferences. Tucking him into bed at night after a story.

But she didn't want to entertain those fantasies now.

She wasn't fit.

Had nothing to offer him.

She couldn't get the hotel concierge out of her mind. Wondered if he could assist on scoring her a teener and a pipe.

Three times, she started down to the lobby.

Three times, she stopped herself.

It was the memory of the Atlanta motel that kept turning her back. The image of her skeletal reflection in that cracked mirror. The idea of someone someday having to tell her son how his mother had OD'd when he was six years old.

In the afternoon, Letty moved to the other side of the roof. She passed in and out of sleep as the sun dropped. In her waking moments, she tried on three promises to herself, just to see how they fit.

I will set up a trust fund for Jacob with half the money and make it so I can never touch it.

I will check myself into the best rehab program I can find.

If I'm still clean a year from now, then, and only then, will I go to my son.

The next time she awoke, there were people all around her and the sun was halfway into the ocean. Letty sat up, came slowly to her feet. She walked over to the edge of the roof.

The people around her were making toasts to the sunset and to each other. Nearby, a woman mentioned a news report concerning the death of John Fitch. The group laughed, someone speculating that the coward had taken his own life.

Letty clutched the railing.

She couldn't escape the idea that it meant something that she'd stayed up here all day. That she'd watched the sun rise, cross the sky and go back into the sea. She hadn't felt this rested in months, and those promises were looking better and better.

Like something she could own.

Keep.

Maybe even live for.

She knew the feeling might not last.

Knew she might fall down again.

But in this moment, Letty felt like the tallest thing on the island.

BLAKE CROUCH has published ten novels, as well as many novellas and short stories. His stories have appeared in *Ellery Queen, Alfred Hitchcock's Mystery Magazine, Thriller* 2, and other anthologies. His novels *Fully Loaded, Run,* and *Stirred* have each earned spots in the top ten of the Kindle bestseller list, and much of his work has been optioned for film. He lives today in Durango, Colorado.